FUNNY LITTLE SOCKS

SARAH L. BARROW

Edition : Culturea (Hérault, 34)
Contact : infos@culturea.fr
Print in Germany by Books on Demand
Design and layout : Derek Murphy
Layout : Reedsy (https://reedsy.com/)
ISBN : 9791041819386
Légal deposit : July 2023

Funny Little Socks

LITTLE MOTHER.

ONE day Kitty's mother called her little daughter to her, and taking both her dimpled dots of hands in her own soft white ones, said, "Kitty, my darling, I am going to New York this morning, to see your dear grandma', and I shall have to leave the house in your charge until I come back. Do you think you can be my little housekeeper for to-day?"

"Oh yes, mamma! I should like that so much! I will keep house as well as you—that is, 'most, not quite!" and Kitty jumped up and down for joy at being trusted with such important affairs.

"You must take care of dear little Luly and Walter, you know; see that they have their dinners fixed right, and go out walking with them and nurse; and if any company comes, you must go down and see them, and say that mamma has gone to New York, will you?"

"Yes, mamma; I will be just as good as pie!" said Kitty, earnestly; "Luly and Wawa will like to have me for a mother, I guess."

"Yes; you are their Little Mother for to-day," said her mamma. "I know you love me, Kitty, and want to save me all the trouble you can; it will be a great comfort to me, while I am away, to feel that I can trust you perfectly;" and she kissed the little, rosy cheek, I'm sure I can't tell how many times, and Kitty felt so proud and happy that she only wished she had been trusted with a much larger family of little brothers and sisters, instead of two; that she might show the more what an excellent Little Mother she intended to be. You would wish so too, wouldn't you! yes, of course!

Kitty May lived with her papa and mamma, Luly and Walter, Mary the nurse, and Betty the cook, three brown horses, two red cows, a black dog, and a white kitten, at a beautiful country seat up the Hudson River. She was only eight years old, but her obedience to her parents, and tender, loving care of her little brother and sister, were beautiful to see, and a shining example to some little girls I know. On the day that I am telling you about, her papa had gone to town, as usual, early in the morning, and now here was mamma going too, and Kitty would be left to play lady of the house as grand as anything.

Well, the carriage was brought to the door, and mamma got in, after kissing her little family all round about twenty times. Everybody rushed to the front piazza to bid her good-by in their own fashion. Trip, the black dog, jumped and barked around the horses, until they nearly kicked him, when he sprang away, snapping out, "No, you don't! no, you don't!" Dody, the white kitten, so called by Walter for "Daisy," mewed as hard as she could from Luly's arms. Walter crowed and chuckled, and said, "Boobi!" meaning good-by; Luly lisped, "Dood-by, dear mamma, div my yove to gan'ma;" and Kitty said, "Good-by, mamma; I'll be a famous Little Mother—see if I'm not!" And so the carriage drove away.

When it was quite out of sight, the little girls skipped and climbed, and wee Walter was carried by nurse up stairs into the nursery; and Kitty said, "Now, Mary, you can just go on with your sewing; you needn't mind us a bit. I'm going to take care of the children; mamma said so."

"Very well, Miss Kitty," said Mary; "I'll sit in the window here, and if you want me, you can call."

So Mary fixed little Walter in his chair, and Luly got hers, and Kitty sat down in her mamma's rocking chair, to be grander.

Walter's chair had a little tray fastened before it, on which his toys were put. His dearest plaything was a ridiculous old doll, with no eyes, half a wig, such a dilapidated pair of kid arms that the stuffing came bursting through in every direction, making her look as if she had a cotton plantation inside her, and the bolls were sprouting out; and such an extremely short pair of legs in proportion to her body, that it seemed as if they must shut into her like a pair of telescopes. Besides this, there was a stale sugar peacock without a tail, a monkey that ran up and down a stick, and a woolly dog that could open his mouth and bark when you pressed him underneath; but the doll was the prime favorite, after all. Walter called her Gawow, and as nobody in the house could imagine what he meant by it, it was supposed to be a pure piece of invention, and a very fine sort of thing.

The children played on peaceably together for some time, when all at once there came a ring at the bell.

"Dear me!" cried Kitty, springing up and smoothing down her little black silk apron in a great flurry. "There comes company, and I'm to go and see them."

"Ou!" said Luly; "me want to see tompany too!"

"And so you shall, you little darling!" said Kitty, kissing her; and, sure enough, up came Ellen, the waiter, to say that the good minister, Mr. Lacy, was down stairs; for Mrs. May had smilingly told her, before she went, that "Miss Kitty would see any one who called."

In high glee, yet somewhat awed by her grown-up dignity, Kitty let Mary brush her soft brown braided wig and Luly's golden curly one; then she rushed into her mother's room in a hurry, called Luly out into the entry, and the little sisters took hold of hands and went down stairs to see the company.

Mr. Lacy was sitting by the window, looking out on the beautiful garden, and did not know the children had entered until he felt a mite of a hand put softly on his, and heard two little pipy voices saying, "How do you do, Mr. Lacy?" The minister turned round and burst right out laughing! for Kitty, when she ran into her mother's room, had put on—what do you think?—why, one of mamma's caps, which was lying on the dressing table! and the queer little thing looked so funny with the lace cap perched on top of her head, that Mr. Lacy laughed heartily, and said, "Why, Kitty! are you the old woman that lived in a shoe? or have you got bald all of a sudden, that you have taken to caps?"

"Oh, I'm Little Mother!" said Kitty; "mamma has gone to the city, and left me to take care of the children, and the house, and Dody, and Trip, until she comes back; and I'm Little Mother to all of them."

"Well, Little Mother," said Mr. Lacy, who was none of your cross, crabbed old ministers, with faces as sour as vinegar, and voices as sharp as a needle, who frighten children half out of their wits, forgetful that "of such is the kingdom of heaven;" "I hope your children will be well brought up, and learn all they should. What does this one know?" lifting Luly to his knee.

"I know 'ittle hymn," said Luly, smiling up confidently in his face.

"Can't you say it for me?" asked the minister. "What is it all about?"

"'Bout 'at a 'ittle child can do," lisped Luly.

"Say it, Luly," said Kitty.

Luly folded her cunning fat hands over each other, and crossed her feet. Then she looked up sideways in Mr. Lacy's face, and sucked her tongue a little bit, and at last, all at once, in a little singing voice, she began:

"I'm a very 'ittle maid;
Hardly can I talk, 'tis true;
Yet mamma I'd love to aid—
What can 'ittle Luly do?

"I can go, on busy feet,
Errands for her all day through;
Work for her, I feel, is sweet—
This can 'ittle Luly do!

"I can hold the gate long skein
When 'tis tangled and askew;
Never wanting to compain[A]—
This can 'ittle Luly do!

"I can search, her book to find,

And be glad to do it, too!

I can always quickly mind—

This can 'ittle Luly do!

"I can ever go up stairs

Cheerfully, when falls the dew;

And with yev'yence say my prayers—

This can 'ittle Luly do!

"GOD will help me, if I try;

He good children loves to view;

Dear Lord Jesus, from on high,

Pease tell Luly what to do!"

"Ah! that is a beautiful hymn," said the good minister. "Don't you know any, Little Mother?"

"I am learning a beautiful hymn," said Kitty, "but I don't know it yet—not quite."

"No?" said Mr. Lacy. "Then I shall have to tell you something myself, I declare. Here, sit down beside me, and listen very attentively."

Now, what do you think the minister told them? "Some dreadful, dismal story, full of dreadful, wicked children, who were sent to prison, I suppose; or an account of how, if they ever dared to run down stairs, or look out of the window, or sneeze in church, on Sundays, they never would get to Heaven!" perhaps you will say. Not a bit of it. He just trotted Luly up and down on his knee, and told them these funny verses:

"Three little kittens from home ran away,

Oh dear! oh dear!

And did you not hear

All that befell them on that day?

Dilly, and Dolly, and Poppledy-polly—

Did you ever hear, in your life, of such folly!

"Out they ran from their mother's door,

And skipped, and tripped,

And danced, and dipped,

Way down the road, where they'd ne'er been before!
Dilly, and Dolly, and Poppledy-polly,
Oh deary! what will be the end of their folly?
"'Come let us go into this barn for mice!'
'Oh don't!' 'Oh stuff!
I'm hungry enough
To eat anything that is sav'ry and nice!'
So quoth little Dolly and Poppledy-polly,
While Dilly looked on, quite aghast at their folly!
"So in it they went, quite full of their fun,
And stared, and glared,
And meauoed, and scared
The poor little mice till they made them all run!
Dilly, and Dolly, and Poppledy-polly;
For Dilly, I'm sorry to say, shared their folly.
"But, alas! while the kittens were hunting up mice,
And munching, and crunching
Their smoking-hot lunching,

A boy came and caught them all up in a trice!
Dilly, and Dolly, and Poppledy-polly;
Oh! OH! OH! what a shocking climax to their folly!
"Oh, how they struggled and mewed in their fright!
And scratched, and snatched
At the dismal old patched
Bag they were thrust into, twisted up tight!
Dilly, and Dolly, and Poppledy-polly;
I warrant, they felt bad enough for their folly.
"Soon to a stranger house they came;
'Oh, ma'! oh, ma'!

Now, only see thar!'

Their captor cried out to an elderly dame;

While Dilly, and Dolly, and Poppledy-polly

Pricked up their ears, and lamented their folly.

"'What, have you brought in a parcel of cats?

Go straight to the pond

And get 'em all drowned!!

I won't have them here, I can tell you; now s'cats!'

Poor Dilly, and Dolly, and Poppledy-polly

Set up a loud howl of distress at their folly!

"Off scampered the boy till he came to the bank

Of a very deep pool;

Oh, wasn't it cruel!

And tossed in the bag!! To the bottom it sank!!!

With Dilly (oh!), and Dolly (oh!), and Poppledy-polly (oh! oh!),

And that was the end of their fun and their folly!"

MORAL.

"So, children, I solemnly beg and implore,

Whatever you do,

(And you're torments a few,)

You'll never slip out of your dear mother's door;

Or, like Dilly, and Dolly, and Poppledy-polly,

You'll surely be made to repent of your folly!"

The children were very much amused with this woful history, bursting out laughing without any kind of fail when Poppledy-polly, of comical memory and name, was mentioned. Luly said, "Oh, me yike that name! me want to call Dody Popply-polly." This made Kitty laugh more than ever, and they had a great time chasing Dody round the hall, and catching her, to bawl in her ears "Poppledy-polly!" by way of kindly informing her that was to be her new name.

Dody didn't seem to like it much, for she jumped out of Luly's arms with a squeal and a flourish of her long tail, and scampered off faster than ever each time. After watching them, and laughing for a while, Mr. Lacy rose to go, saying:

"Good-by, Little Mother; I must go and see some of the big mothers now. Don't forget me on any account, and tell your mamma, when she comes home, that I approve your style of housekeeping very much indeed."

"Good-by, Mr. Lacy," said Kitty. "Thank you for your funny story."

"Tank 'ou—funny 'tory!" repeated Luly after her sister.

Mr. Lacy lifted the little thing up to his shoulder, and held her there a minute, saying, "Good-by, Poppledy-polly! I hope, when I come again, you will know another hymn to say."

Luly didn't like much to be called Poppledy-polly, and she said, with an air of considerable displeasure, "My name Luly May;" but when the minister kissed her, and called her "his little lamb," she relented, and cooed, "Me yove 'ou, miniter!'

Then something quite sorrowful happened; for two great tears gathered in the minister's eyes, and came slowly rolling down his kind face. Ah! he thought of his own little pet lamb, who once lisped, too, "Me yove 'ou;" who said so now to the dear Jesus; and with that last thought came comfort. Floy was only "sleeping"—and setting little Luly gently down, Mr. Lacy laid a hand on each childish head, saying, "God bless you, my little lambs," and went quietly away. The children watched him drive off, and then capturing Dody once more—by the end of her tail this time—Kitty popped her in her apron; and lugged her up stairs in triumph.

There they found Wawa, sitting on the floor, with an immense pair of scissors held in both hands, and an expression of extreme horror on his face. Mary had left the room, and Kitty, running up to her baby brother, pulled away the scissors in a great fright, exclaiming, "Why, Wawa! where did you get those?"

Wawa stared astonished for a moment, his great blue eyes opened very wide indeed; then he bubbled out, "On yer fore (floor); yook! Gawow all poil!" (spoiled); and poor Wawa puckered up his little rosy mouth, and began to cry most piteously.

Luly popped on the floor beside him in a minute, and pulling his curly head down on her breast, she murmured, "There—don't c'y, never matter, dear bedder—s'eel get well!" while Kitty lifted up poor Gawow, who was indeed in a pitiable condition. Walter had ornamented her face with several deep digs of the scissors, which made her look as if she had been to the wars and come home with a number of bullet holes in her. Then, not satisfied with this—what does that monkey Wawa do but rip up her whole body from the neck to the waist, and shake out every bit of the bran all over the carpet! leaving the wretched Gawow with not the least particle of insides.

Did you ever hear of such a piece of mischief? But then Walter was such a little fellow—not quite two years old; of course he didn't mean to do anything wrong, and nobody thought of blaming him; so Kitty called Mary to come and sweep up the bran, and Luly and Walter were soon happily engaged in stuffing Gawow with rags, making her look as good as new—or as good as old, I might say; for she was such a direful object in the first place, that it seemed as though she must have been bought in that condition, and never could have been otherwise; after which they dressed her in her very best bonnet and frock, and treated her to a nice dance in the garden, all taking hold of hands; until Mary looked out of the window and called them to come up to dinner.

Kitty was old enough, now, to dine with the grown folks, and behaved like a perfect little lady, too; but on this occasion she was going to take early dinner in the nursery.

She and Luly helped Mary pull out the nursery table, and set the three little plates upon it. Walter's dinner was some mashed potato, with just a tiny mite of chicken among it, minced very fine, and made into an elegant hill on his plate, and a "wishing bone" to suck. Luly had the same, only with more chicken; and Kitty cut up her own wing and slice of breast, with her particular knife and fork, as nice as you please.

There was a great deal of merriment over the dinner, when Walter would look away just as Mary gave him a spoonful of potato, watching her out of the corner of his eye, though, and then bob round again and say "Feed!" just as she had put it down, thinking he didn't want any more. Then he insisted on making Gawow taste the wishing bone, and poked it into both her eyes in succession, as if that was the usual way for people to eat things. After they had finished the chicken and potato, they had some nice custard pudding; and when dinner was over, Kitty went right to the wash stand and cleaned her teeth, while Luly held up her mouth to have Mary brush her little pearly teeth. Do you always do this, little reader? If not, let me beg you to begin right away. Are they done now? Very well, then let us go on with the story.

Pretty soon after, the children were dressed to go out walking; for it was in the early spring time when all this happened, and still pleasant, in the cold country, to take the middle of the day for going out. So Kitty and Luly had their little blue poplin "coat-dresses" buttoned on, and the soft white woollen hoods tied under their rosy faces, and Walter was decked out in his new blue coat; which pleased him so much that he distinguished himself immediately afterward by walking all alone away from the door to the window, quite across the room, and there sitting down suddenly on the floor, much to his astonishment. At last they were all ready and started off, Kitty and Luly hand in hand, and Walter in his little carriage.

The road they liked best led along the top of a high bank, and was called "Buena Vista" terrace. There were very pretty houses built along here, shaded by tall trees;

and if the children peeped cautiously over the iron fence that guarded the edge of the bank, they could sometimes see the steam cars rushing along the shore below. They were very fond of watching the hurrying train go by, though it frightened them a little, particularly when the engine gave a shrill scream before stopping at the station about a quarter of a mile further on. Kitty and Luly couldn't help squealing too when that happened, and then laughing very much, and scampering on, playing they were steam engines.

Just as they were passing by the prettiest house on the terrace, out came a young lady that Kitty and Luly knew and loved dearly, with a "tremendous dog" stalking slowly after her.

"Why, Kitty!" she cried, "is that you? Nurse, do bring the children in. I want to see them so much!"

So Mary went to open the gate; but before she could do so, up marched Buffo, the "tremendous dog," and lifted the latch with his nose! Oh, how Kitty and Luly did laugh and clap their hands! but their enjoyment and surprise were at full height when the kind young lady, whom they called Miss Ella, lifted Luly, and Mary held Wawa, on Buffo's shaggy back, and the good fellow carried them both safely to the house. Wawa crowed and laughed, and drummed with his heels against the side of his charger; but the brave dog never tried to shake him off, and just walked gravely along, looking as trustworthy as possible. Then, when the little children got off, Kitty mounted somewhat fearfully on Buffo's broad back, and rode all around the grass plot, laughing with delight.

After that, Miss Ella made them sit down in a great rocking chair on the porch, wide enough for all three to get in at once, and asked them what they had been doing that morning; and then Kitty told about her being Little Mother, and Luly said, so funny, "Miniter tome see Luly and Kitty, and tell funny 'tory 'bout Dilly, and Dolly, and Popply-polly; and 'en—and 'en I talled Dody Popply-polly, and s'e wan away!"

That amused Miss Ella very much, and pretty soon she opened her work-box, took out a paper of lemon drops, and gave Luly, and Kitty, and Wawa each a handful. Luly was a generous little puss, and wanted every one to share her "goodies;" so she even offered a lemon drop to Buffo, when, what do you think the great black fellow did? He just put his great fore paws on Luly's lap, opened his wide red mouth, and eat up every one of the drops at a mouthful!

Poor Luly opened her mouth in rueful astonishment, and looked very much as if she was going to burst out crying; but Miss Ella consoled her by giving her some more drops, and Wawa thrust one of his into her mouth, saying, "Dog eat Luly's d'ops; Wawa torry."

So they talked away till it was time to go; and then Miss Ella kissed her little visitors; and Buffo wanted to kiss them too, with his warm red tongue; but Luly took good care to be out of the way this time. I expect the little thing thought he would eat her up like a lemon drop; so Kitty let him lick her hand instead; and then Buffo let Miss Ella put Luly and Wawa on his back again, and rode them down to the gate, where they bid good-by to their kind friend.

Tea was ready for them when they came back, and "when fell the dew" Luly and Kitty went "cheerfully up stairs" to bed. And now a sweet, serious expression came over Little Mother's face, and her great brown eyes were filled with loving reverence, as Luly, in her little white night gown, bent her golden curls on the lap of her sister, and lisped out "Now I yay me down to s'eep"—that dear, precious little verse that I think all the children in the world must say; and prayed "Dear Jesus" to "b'ess papa and mamma, and dear sister, and 'ittle bedder, and mate Luly dood 'ittle child;" and as Little Mother's lips were murmuring those words after her, the door opened, and there stood her own dear mamma and papa, just home from the city; and oh! I can't tell you half how much they loved their darling ones when they saw that sweet little scene.

And then there was a merry frolic with papa, who rode Luly and Wawa on both shoulders as well as Buffo did; and a happy time with dear mamma, who brought them three great oranges from grandma', and ever so many kisses for her share; and a holy, blessed time when that dear mamma knelt by her precious Kitty's bedside, and prayed God to bless and keep

DOLLS AT HOUSEKEEPING.

OF all the sweet little ten-year old maidens that ever laughed and danced through their happy lives, I don't suppose one had such a wonderful doll's house, or such a fine family of dolls, as Lina. Let me describe the family and their residence.

In one of the upper rooms of Lina's house you would see, if you happened to walk in, another whole house built. It is two stories high: its front is red brick; and a flight of brown stone steps, made of sand-paper glued over wood, leads up to the entrance. It has real sashes in the windows, which open French fashion; a silver door-plate, with the name of "Montague" upon it; and a little mat, about as large as a half dollar, on the upper step! If we could make ourselves as small as dolls, we might walk in, and find out that the hall has a dark wood floor, some cunning little pictures hanging on the wall, a noble black walnut staircase, and is lighted with a real little hall lamp.

The parlor, on one side of this hall, has a velvet carpet on the floor, satin chairs and sofas, a centre table covered with tiny books, an étagere full of ornaments, and a wicker-work flower stand filled with flowers. Real little mantel and pier glasses are over the fire place, and between the front windows, which are hung with elegant lace curtains; and there is, besides, a piano-forte, a gold chandelier stuck full of china wax-candles, and a little clock that can wind up—though as to its going, that has to be imagined, for it obstinately represents the time as a quarter to twelve, morning, noon, and night!

On the opposite side of the hall is the dining-room. It is furnished with a fine side-board, holding a silver tea-set and some tiny glass goblets and decanters; a round table, which is abominably disorderly, it must be confessed, being spread with a table cloth all awry, and covered with a granddinner of wooden chickens and vegetables of various sorts; a mould of yellow-glass jelly, and a pair of fancy fruit dishes, made of cream candy. The dining-room chairs, with real leather seats, are scattered about, and there is even the daily newspaper thrown down on the floor, where the master of the house may have left it! Up stairs there are three bedrooms, furnished in the same fashionable style; and, in short, such an elegant doll's house is not to be found anywhere but in a French toy shop. This one was brought from Paris by Lina's elder brother, and set up in this very room last Christmas as a surprise for his dear little sister. But it is time I should describe the family who lived in this elegant mansion. So, little reader, if you will only take fast hold of the end of the author's pen, shut up your eyes tight, and then open them very quick on this page, heigh! presto! you and she will be turned into little personages just the size of dolls, able to walk up the brown stone steps, enter the house, and take a peep at the Montague family.

On a lounge by the parlor fire sits an elegant lady, who is rather skimpy about the wig, and therefore holds the honorable post of mamma to the family; as this circumstance, combined with her looking excessively inky about the nose, gives her a somewhat aged and anxious appearance. She wears a blue silk dress with five flounces, a lace cap, and a watch and chain; and her name is Mrs. Charles Augustus Montague. Her husband, Mr.Charles Augustus, is a china doll with a crop of rather scrubby flaxen hair, which can be combed and brushed as much as Lina chooses. Although he is so rich, he has only one suit of clothes, and must even go to parties in a pair of checked gingham trowsers, a red vest, and a blue coat with brass buttons! He is supposed to be down town at present, which circumstance is represented by his being unceremoniously thrust into a corner upside down.

Several smaller wax and china boys and girls represent the family of the ill-used Mr. Montague; but the belle of the whole doll-community is his eldest daughter, Miss Isabella Belmont Montague. She is a waxen young lady of the most splendid description; her hair is arranged like the empress', whom, indeed, she greatly resembles; her feet and hands are of wax, and she has more dresses than I can possibly count. I am afraid you will scarcely believe me, but she actually has a real little ermine muff and tippet, a pair of india-rubbers, an umbrella, a camels' hair shawl, and real corsets! and was won, with all her wardrobe, at one of the raffles in the great Union Bazaar. You went there, didn't you—you cunning little kitten? and saw all the dolls? I hope you got one too, so I do, certainly!

Besides the Montague family, there is a numerous colony of other dolls; but they, poor things, live in any corner where Lina chooses to put them; and all day Sunday are shut up in a dark closet, with nothing to do but count their fingers and toes, if they can contrive to see them; though they have nearly as fine a wardrobe—for Lina's great amusement, next to playing with the whole colony, is to make new dresses for them.

One Saturday afternoon, Lina was playing with her dolls in the baby house, with two of her little neighbors, Minnie and Maggie Elliott, to keep her company. It was a dark, rainy sort of day; but what difference did that make to the children? They never wanted to make a parcel of stupid morning calls, or go out shopping and spend all their money on silly finery; no—they were full of their play in the house, and didn't care a doll's shoe-string how hard it rained.

"Oh, dear!" said Lina at last; "seems to me this play is getting very stupid! I wish we knew something else to play at but everlasting 'house!'"

"I'll tell you what would be great fun!" said little Minnie, looking wise. "You know, Lina, we spent a week once in the country with 'Alice Nightcaps;' and her sister, 'Aunt Fanny's' daughter, showed us such a nice, funny play! Instead of our being mothers, and aunts, and fathers, and the dolls our children, the dolls were all the people themselves, and we moved them about and spoke for them."

"Yes, it was such a nice plan!" said Maggie; "you can't think, Lina. Suppose we divide these dolls into families, and play that Miss Isabella Belmont Montague was going to be married, and all about it."

"Oh, yes! yes! that will be splendid!" cried Lina. "Whom will you manage, Maggie?"

"I'd rather have Miss Isabella," said Maggie.

"And I want Mr. Morris," said Minnie. "He shall be the lover."

"Very well, then I'll make the father and mother talk," said Lina, generously taking the less splendid dolls, without a word of mean complaint, such as "There, you hateful thing, you always want the best;" or, "I do wish I could do as I like with my own dolls!" forgetting that company must be allowed to take the best always. The other dolls were equally divided between the children, and then Lina exclaimed, with a delighted little skip in the air, "Now, we are all ready to begin! Come, girls, what time shall it be?"

"Oh, have them at breakfast!" chimed both the little visitors; and so, in defiance of the parlor clock, the time of day was supposed to be eight in the morning. The children, with many little chuckling pauses, while they considered what to do next, twitched the unlucky table cloth straight, put the tea-set on the table, and gave the family a wooden beefsteak for breakfast, and a large plateful of wooden buttered toast, which came from a box full of such indigestible dainties. Then they fished Mr. Charles Augustus Montague out of the corner, and set him upright in a chair at the head of the table, with his newspaper fastened in his hands, by having a couple of large pins stuck through it and them. The points of the pins showed on the other side, and looked as if he had a few extra finger nails growing on the backs of his hands. Quite a curiosity he'd have been for Barnum's Museum,wouldn't he? you precious little old toad.

Mrs. Montague was seated behind the tea-tray, and Miss Isabella was reclining on a sofa up stairs, as if she was too lazy to come down when the rest of the family did. As the front door was only large enough for the dolls, the whole back of the house came away. Lina and her visitors delightedly sat down cross-legged on the floor behind it, and the play began, the children talking for the dolls.

MRS. MONTAGUE. (Lina speaks for her in a fine voice.) I wish you would lay down your paper a moment, Charles; I want to speak to you.

MR. M. Well, my dear, I am listening.

MRS. M. No, you are not; put down the paper! [As this couldn't very well be done by the gentleman himself, Maggie twitched it away for him, and threw it under the table.]

MRS. M. Now, Charles, I must say I think it is high time Isabella was married. She is most six months old, I declare! and it strikes me we had better see if we can find her a husband.

MR. M. What you say is very sensible, my dear; so I will call to-day on my friend Mr. Morris, and invite him to dinner. Perhaps they will fall in love with each other.

MRS. M. Oh! but is he handsome, Mr. Montague?

MR. M. Handsome! I should rather think so! Why, he is nearly two feet high, with curly black hair; a nose that can be seen at the side—which is more than yours can be, Mrs. Montague—and eyes which open and shut of themselves when he lies down or sits up. Then he is a Seventh Regimenter, too, and always wears his uniform; which makes him look very genteel.

MRS. M. Oh, I am sure he must be lovely! Do bring him to dinner this very day.

Here Maggie made the dining-room door open, and in walked Miss Isabella. She wore a pink merino morning dress, open in front, to show her embroidered petticoat, a pair of bronze slippers with pink bows, and a net with steel beads in it. Maggie set her down hard in one of the chairs, and pushed her up to the table; while Minnie, who moved the nigger boy doll, who waited on table, picked him up by his woolly top-knot, from the floor, where he had tumbled, and made him hand the young lady a cup of tea. Then Maggie began:

MISS ISABELLA. Dear me, mamma! this tea's as cold as a stone! I wish you would have breakfast a little later; as I'm so tired when I come home from a party, that I can't think of getting up at seven o'clock.

MRS. M. But you must get up, my love. Besides, we want plenty of time to-day, so's we can be ready; for we are going to have company to dinner.

ISABELLA. Who is coming, mamma?

MRS. M. Mr. Morris, my dear.

ISABELLA. Oh, I am so glad!

MRS. M. Yes, you're going to be married to-morrow, my dear; we will invite all our relations and friends, and you must have a white satin wedding dress; you certainly must.

ISABELLA. How nice! S'pose we go out and buy it now.

MRS. M. We can't go to-day; it's our eceptin (reception) day, you know.

MR. M. Well, I 'spect I must go down town. Good-by, my dears. I shall certainly ask Mr. Morris to dinner. He's a very nice young man for a small dinner party.

So the children made Mr. Montague kiss his wife and daughter; which they did by bumping his china nose against their cheeks, until it nearly made a dent in the wax; and then pranced him down the front steps, and put him in his corner again.

Then Minnie's doll came in. She took up Mr. Morris, a composition doll, in a Seventh Regiment uniform, who had been bought at a fair, and began moving him across the floor until he was opposite the door. Then she commenced talking.

MR. MORRIS. Why, I declare! here is Mr. Montague's house. I think I will go in and make a call.

And he ran up the steps, and pretended to ring the bell; but as it was only a handle, Lina rang the dinner bell instead.

MR. MORRIS. It's very funny they don't answer the bell! (Ting-a-ling-ling.) Come! make haste, I want to get in.

Here Minnie took up Toby, the black boy, carried him to the front door, and kindly opened it for him.

TOBY. Laws, massa! is dat you? I was jus' tastin' de jolly, to be sure it was good for dinner! so I couldn't come no sooner.

MR. MORRIS. Is Miss Isabella Belmont Montague at home?

TOBY. Yes, massa, de ladies is to hum; walk in de parlor.

So Mr. Morris came in (with Minnie's hand behind him), and sat down on the sofa. It was rather small for him, and he covered it up so much that there wasn't a bit of room for Miss Isabella, when she came down. Maggie had dressed her meanwhile in her green silk skirt, which had real little three-cornered pockets, with an embroidered pocket handkerchief sticking out of one, and her white tucked waist.

Up jumped Mr. Morris, and made her such an elegant bow, that his cap, which he was obliged to keep on all the time, in consequence of the strap being glued fast under his chin, fell all to one side; and looked as if the top of his head had accidentally come off and been stuck on crooked.

MR. MORRIS. Good morning, Miss Isabella; how do you do?

Isabella. Very well, thank you. How do you do, Mr. Morris?

MR. MORRIS. Oh, Miss Isabella, I should be quite well if I hadn't sitch a pain in my heart!

ISABELLA. A pain in your heart! What makes you have that, Mr. Morris?

MR. MORRIS. YOU!

ISABELLA. I!

MR. MORRIS. Oh, Miss Isabella, you can't think how I adore you! I love you so much that it makes my eyes shut up when I don't want them to; and my heart beats so that it shakes my cap all to one side!

ISABELLA. Dear me, Mr. Morris, you are quite afflitted! but never mind—papa is going to have you to dinner to-day; you'd better go right down town, so he can ask you.

MR. MORRIS. But I can't eat any dinner, Miss Isabella, without you will marry me!

Here Minnie tried to make Mr. Morris pop down on his knees; but as he wasn't a jointed doll, he lost his balance, and tumbled flat on his face instead.

MISS ISABELLA. Here, what are you doing? get up, do, and stop your noise! [For Minnie couldn't help a long-sounding o—h! when her doll floppeddown. So Maggie made the young lady catch hold of Mr. Morris's shoulder straps and help twitch him on the sofa again, to go on with his proposal.]

MR. MORRIS. Will you marry me, Miss Isabella? I'm such a nice young man—you don't know—and we'll live in a real pretty house.

MISS ISABELLA. No, I can't marry you till after you have come to dinner; mamma said so.

MR. MORRIS. Well, then, I must wait; but only say that you will have me.

ISABELLA. Oh, yes!

At this point the children laid down the dolls and broke into such a merry trill of laughter, that it would have done anybody's heart good to hearthem. It seemed so funny to have the dolls making love in this fashion, they couldn't help it. As soon as they were sober again, the play went on thus:

MR. MORRIS. Well, Miss Isabella, I b'lieve I must go now; I've got an old sister at home, who will scold me if I don't come back. Can't you 'vite her too? She has a pretty bad time, poor thing! 'cause she is so oldy that she is kept on a shelf till she's all dusty. Her wig is dreadful fuzzy, and some of it comes out and stands up at the top. But I'll dust her well and stick a pin in her wig to keep it on, and make her look real nice, if you'll only ask her.

ISABELLA. Well, I guess she can come; but she must have a new dress for the wedding.

MR. MORRIS. Yes, she shall, certainly. Good-by, Miss Isabella. I'm going down town pretty soon, so your father can ask me to come.

MISS ISABELLA. Oh yes, do! I want you to come velly much.

"Now, Maggie, we must stop the play a little while," said Lina, "and fix the dinner for them."

"Yes, do," cried Maggie; "let's see, what shall be for dinner?"

"Oh, chicken, that's the nicest!" said Minnie.

"No, they had chicken yesterday," said Lina; "let them have roast beef."

"Very well," went on Maggie, who was looking over the dishes in the box of "eatables," as Lina called them. "Roast beef, mashed potatoes, and macaroni."

"Oh, not macaroni," cried Minnie; "the cheese will bite their tongues."

"Oh, yes! Mr. Morris likes macaroni," said her sister.

"Well, macaroni, then; and plum-pudding for dessert—and apples."

"Ah, make them have jelly," said Lina; "that's the prettiest thing in the box."

So the dinner was hunted out, and the three children set the table in fine style; while Toby, the black boy, whose business it certainly was to have done it, sat coolly in Mr. Montague's armchair, with his master's newspaper in his lap, and goggled at the table without moving an inch. Then Lina dressed Mrs. Montague, and Maggie and Minnie together dressed Miss Isabella; and nobody dressed poor Mr. Morris, or Mr. Charles Augustus Montague; because they unluckily had but one suit a piece, sewed fast on to them at that.

This time Miss Isabella wore a pink silk frock, with a deep puffing round the bottom, finished at each edge with black velvet. Then she had a long pink sash, edged with two rows of narrow black velvet; a pointed belt encircled her waist, and the body of her dress was a mass of puffs, with narrow black velvet between. On her head was a pink wreath, with long ribbon ends hanging down her back; and tied fast to her wrist was a pink feather fan with gold sticks. In fact, Miss Isabella looked rather as if she were going to a party than coming down to dinner; but the children thought the pink silk so charming, that she must wear it, whether or no.

Mrs. Montague wore a purple silk, a black lace shawl, and a head-dress of pink rosebuds and black lace.

When the ladies were fairly seated in the parlor, Lina rang the bell, and Minnie and Maggie made Mr. Morris come in, leading his sister by the hand. She was a dismal object to behold, sure enough! and if she could have blushed for herself, I think she certainly would. She wore a green barègedress, trimmed with flaming red ribbons; some of the gathers were out at the waist, and her petticoat showed at the bottom.

Mr. Morris, or Minnie—I don't know which—had stuck the ends of her wig down for her once, but they had come up again, and looked as if her hair had taken to growing with the roots uppermost. The end of her nose was blacker than Mrs.

Montague's, and her eyes, which moved with a wire like other wax dolls, had got out of order somehow, and remained stationary, with nothing but the whites showing; and, altogether, poor Miss Morris looked like a two-legged rag-bag come home from the wars, with both eyes out, half a nose, and no hair worth mentioning.

Lina made Mr. Montague come home as soon as she was rid of the dinner bell; and after they had all shaken hands until their wax and kid and china wrists must have ached, the company rather unceremoniously marched right into the dining-room. I suppose Mr. Montague was tremendously hungry, and gave his wife's hand a good pinch when he shook it, to make her hurry things up; but, however that may be, they were walked in to dinner in straight order. Mr. Morris sat by Miss Isabella, with his forlorn old sister on the other hand, and as the opposite side of the table looked rather bare, Minnie proposed that some of the children should come down to fill up.

"Oh, yes—and let them be dreadfully naughty and do all sorts of mischief," said Maggie. So Miss Angelina Seraphina Montague, and Master Algernon Pop-eyes Montague (so called because he had glass eyes, which stuck out in a lobster-ish fashion), were sent for in a hurry and brought down by their nurse, a beautiful doll dressed as a French bonne, and Maggie. Algernon wore the costume of a sailor boy, and Angelina was no other than a nun in a black robe! But never mind, they did very well to fill up, and sat smirking at the company very genteelly.

So, then, Lina made Mr. Montague begin.

MR. MONT. Will you take some roast beef, Miss Morris?

ALGERNON. No, papa, help me first!

MR. M. Algy Pop-eyes Montague! be still! Here, Toby, hand Miss Morris her plate.

ALGY. Don't you do it, Toby!

MRS. M. Hush up, you naughty boy!

MR. M. Mr. Morris, here's some meat for you.

MRS. M. Take some macaroni, Mr. Morris; it's real good.

MR. MORRIS. Thank you, ma'am; I think I will.

So the company were helped; though, as the meat and vegetables were glued fast to the dishes they were on, I'm afraid they must have had rather a slim dinner.

Then Maggie went on.

MISS ISABELLA. Mr. Morris, I think I am rather tired of that uniform of yours; it makes you look too high in the neck. When we are married, you ought to have a dress coat.

ANGELINA. H-a! h-a-a-a! he hasn't got any other coat! I wouldn't marry an old goose with only one suit!

MRS. M. For shame, Miss! your father hadn't but one when we were married; but, bless me! what is Algernon doing?

Sure enough, Master Algy was doing something extraordinary, for Maggie had made him overset the dish of potatoes in the middle of the table,and then jump up and sit on the back of his chair, with both legs in the air!

MRS. M. My pasence! what a naughty boy! Toby, take this bad boy right up stairs; I am socked! (shocked.)

ALGY. Oh, boo-hoo! boo-hoo! please let me stay!

MRS. M. Well, then, behave yourself.

MISS MORRIS. Mrs. Montague, I think you had better send your children away; they are too bad for anything.

ANGELINA. Oh! oh! I wouldn't be your child for a dollar! ("That's just what I say to my big sister!" put in Maggie in her proper person.)

MRS. M. Oh, they are dear little things; they only do it in fun, Miss Morris.

MR. MORRIS. Well, I don't see it. If they were my children, I should lock them up in a dark closet.

MISS MORRIS. So should I.

ANGELINA. H-a! h-a-a-a! that's just where you are kept yourself!

MISS MORRIS. Oh, I shall faint!

MRS. M. Angelina! you sha'n't have any pudding for being so bad. There, I guess it's time for dessert,"—and without condescending to ask if the company were through dinner, Mrs. Montague, with a wave of her lily-white kid hand, ordered Toby to clear away the dishes; and, the pudding and jelly being put on the table, Lina went on:

MR. M. Miss Morris, have some plum-pudding?

TOBY. No, take some ob de jolly, missis; he so jolly good! I taste um!

Mr. M. Toby, I am astonissed! I shall have to discharge you to-morrow.

"And have an Irishman come!" cried Minnie; "and talk funny, like our Patrick!"

"Yes, that will be real fun!" said Lina. "There, they have had dinner enough; let them go in the parlor now."

Accordingly, the company had their chairs pushed back for them and were taken into the parlor, all but the naughty children, who had to be sent straight to bed, they were so bad. Mr. and Mrs. Montague took possession of the arm chairs, as they were the oldest; Miss Morris wasaccommodated with an uncommonly hard ottoman without any back, in the corner; Mr. Morris plumped down on the sofa, as that was the only seat large enough for him, and the play went on (Minnie speaking).

MR. MORRIS. Miss Isabella, I wish you would sing us a song.

ISABELLA. Oh, really, I have sitch a bad cold. I don't think I can.

MR. MORRIS. Oh, please do, Miss Isabella! Sing that pretty song about the little milkmaid.

ISABELLA. Well, I'll see if I can.

So Maggie made the young lady take a funny little scrap of music out of the stand (called a Canterbury), and put it on the piano. The title of the piece on the outside was, "Souvenirs de l'Opera," which means in English "Recollections of the Opera," but it did just as well for a song. Miss Isabella was seated at the piano, and Maggie moved her hands up and down the keys, to look as if she were playing; while in her own sweet bird-like voice she sang for her this song:

"'Where are you going, my pretty maid?

Where are you going, my pretty maid?'

'I'm going a milking, sir,' she said,

'I'm going a milking, sir,' she said.

"'May I go with you, my pretty maid?

May I go with you, my pretty maid?'

'Yes, if you please, kind sir,' she said,

'Yes, if you please, kind sir,' she said.

"'What is your father, my pretty maid?

What is your father, my pretty maid?'

'My father's a farmer, sir,' she said,

'My father's a farmer, sir,' she said.

"'Oh, then may I marry you, my pretty maid?

Then may I marry you, my pretty maid?'

'Yes, if you please, kind sir,' she said,

'Yes, if you please, kind sir,' she said.

"'What is your fortune, my pretty maid?

What is your fortune, my pretty maid?'

'My face is my fortune, sir,' she said,

'My face is my fortune, sir,' she said.

"'Oh, then I can't marry you, my pretty maid!

But then I won't marry you, my pretty maid!'

'Nobody asked you, sir!' she said,

'NOBODY ASKED YOU, SIR!!' she said!"

The dolls all clapped their hands very hard when Miss Isabella finished singing, as if they liked it "first rate." Mr. Morris leaned back so far in hisseat, either from admiration or because he was slipping off, that his eyes suddenly shut up, and opened with a queer little pop inside of him when Minnie righted him. As to Miss Morris, she glared at the company with her old white eyeballs as if she was looking down inside of herself to see how the pudding had agreed with her.

Then Maggie went on.

MISS ISABELLA. There! how do you like that?

MR. MORRIS. Oh, thank you, Miss Isabella; it's the sweetest song I ever heard.

MRS. MONTAGUE. Won't you sing us a song, Mr. Morris?

MR. M. No, I believe I must go now. I have all my things to pack up, so we can start off travelling right away. Come, sister, stick the roots of your hair in, and open your distressed looking eyes, and let us be off home.

"I wonder if her eyes will open?" said Maggie.

"Let's try!" said Lina. "Give the wire a good, hard pull."

As she spoke, she caught hold of the wire and gave a tremendous jerk, when, dreadful to relate, POP! out came poor Miss Morris's eyes completely! and tumbled down somewhere inside of her! leaving two great holes in her head of the most fearful description!

The children stared at her in round-eyed astonishment. Now she was certainly too hideous to come to the wedding; and the little girls tried to look as sorry as they could for her, but it was no use; Miss Morris was such a ridiculous object, that they all three burst into fits of laughing. Lina, who had hold of the poor thing, shook so with glee, that the eyes rattled up and down inside her head like a pack of crackers going off, which made the children laugh still more.

At last Minnie contrived to check herself, and made the brother say, rather unfeelingly:

Mr. Morris. There you go with your eyes out! A pretty figure you've made of yourself.

Miss Isabella. Oh! oh!! OH!!! OH!!!!

MRS. M. Goody, Isabella's got the hysterics! Get some water, quick! what shall I do?

MISS MORRIS. Oh, my eye! my eye! it's sich a pain!

MR. MONTAGUE. Toby, bring some water this minute.

TOBY. (Minnie brings him in with a pitcher.) Here, massa, here de water. My! see de ole woman wid her eye out! ha! ha!

MRS. M. Toby, put down that water, and go 'way.

Minnie accordingly made believe that Toby was pouring water right on the floor; then she turned the pitcher upside down in his hand, and spoke for him.

TOBY. Dere de water, missis.

MRS. M. Oh! it's all over the carpet! How dare you, Toby?

TOBY. Why, missis, you told me to put down de water!

MRS. M. Oh, I shall go distracted!

MR. MORRIS. Come, sister, I 'spect you'd better go home and send for Doctor Bumpstead! Maybe he can fish up your eyes again, and stick them in right side out. A—h! good-by, Miss Isabella, good-by, Mrs. Montague!

ALL THE DOLLS IN CHORUS. Good-by, a—h!

"Oh! did ever anybody have such a funny play before!" cried Lina, fairly dropping Miss Morris, and clapping her hands with delight. "I mean always to play in this way."

"Yes, it is so nice!" said Minnie. "But, come, Lina, how shall we dress Miss Isabella to get married?"

"Oh, she has a wedding-dress all ready," replied Lina; "white silk with lace over."

"Splendid!" cried both the sisters.

"Now, if Mr. Morris could only have a plain suit, he would look so much more like a bridegroom."

"Well, perhaps sister will make him one," said Lina; "but what shall we do with poor Miss Morris?"

The recollection of Miss Morris's mishap set them off again laughing; and finally they decided that she might come to the wedding, but must keep her handkerchief to her eyes all the time, as if she were quite overcome by having her brother married;

as well she might be, for how would her two holes instead of eyes compare with Miss Isabella Belmont Montague's charms?

This point settled, Lina and her little visitors were just beginning to review the other dolls, to see who would look best at the wedding, when a knock came at the door, and in walked Mary, Lina's nurse, to say that Minnie and Maggie were sent for!

"Oh, what a pity!" cried Lina. "I wish you could stay all day, and all night, and all the rest of the time. It's too bad!"

"Oh, that the afternoons were forty-'leven times as long!" said Maggie. "Well, we must go, I suppose. Good-by, Lina; we'll come Monday afternoon, if mamma will let us; and finish the play."

So the children kissed each other, and Minnie and Maggie were bundled up in their warm coats and hoods, and went home. As soon as they were gone, Lina ran to her sister Alice with Mr. Morris, and begged her to make him a suit of black to get married in, as Miss Isabella had expressed her preference for that style of dress. Alice kindly promised she would, and that very evening she hunted up some black cloth that was left from a cloak of her mother's, and in a few hours Mr. Morris was rigged out in the last style of fashion. Here is his carte de visite, taken in his wedding clothes. You see, the photograph man left his own hat on the table by mistake; doesn't it look funny?

It was past Lina's bedtime before Mr. Morris was completely dressed; but she was allowed to sit up "just this once," and when he was finished, she kissed Alice a great many times, carried him off in triumph, and shut him up tight in a box, for fear his clothes should get tumbled.

Monday afternoon, Minnie and Maggie came again, bringing with them a dear little wax doll of Minnie's, and a great paper of sugar-plums, to "play party" with. When Mr. Morris had been sufficiently admired in his new clothes, the children collected theother dolls, and put the Montague family in their house again. Mr. Montague was left all alone in the parlor to receive the company, and the ladies were up stairs in the front bed room. Miss Isabella's wedding dress was spread out on the elegant French bed, all ready for her to wear; and as it is a well-known fact that a fashionable lady cannot possibly get dressed in less than three hours, the time was put at nine o'clock, as the wedding would take place at twelve.

Lina then began the play:

MRS. MONTAGUE. Come, my dear, it is time for you to dress; you've only got three hours to get all ready in.

MISS ISABELLA. Yes, mamma, I am putting on my shoes now. (That is, Maggie was putting them on.) Oh, dear! they are a great deal too tight! they hurt me dreadfully. Please let me take them off.

MRS. M. No, they are not; they are a beautiful fit; don't be silly, Isabella.

ISABELLA. I think you are real mean! There, they are on; now I must put on my dress.

Here Maggie made her stand up, and Lina put on her dress and fastened it.

ISABELLA. Oh, my! what a beautiful dress! Can't I keep it on all the time, mamma?

MRS. M. Why, no; of course not! This is your wedding dress.

ISABELLA. Well, then, I mean to get married over again next year, so I can wear it some more.

MRS. M. Now I must put on your veil, my dear, and then you will be all ready.

Here Maggie clapped her hands to express Miss Isabella's joy, while Lina put on the veil.

ISABELLA. Oh, how pretty I look!

MRS. M. Don't be vain, Isabella. There, you are dressed; sit down now, while I get ready.

So Miss Isabella sat down with her new frock sticking out all around her, like a perfect balloon, a most magnificent creature to behold! Her dress was made of white silk, trimmed all round the bottom with deep blonde lace, which was finished at the top with narrow silver cord. It was looped up on one side with a bouquet of white flowers, with silver leaves, and her waist was covered with a blonde lace bertha, and had a bouquet of the same flowers on the front, called a corsage. She wore a lace veil and a wreath of orange blossoms, and in her hand, tied fast there, was another large bouquet, and a lace-bordered pocket handkerchief. As to Mrs. Montague, she was hardly less splendidly attired, in a mauve silk with eleven flounces, a lace collar and sleeves, and a superb diamond breastpin—made of glass.

Well, dear me, I don't know how I can find room enough to describe all the splendid ladies that came to the wedding. They were none of them quite as elegant as Miss Isabella Belmont Montague, but they all had on their Sunday-go-to-meeting, Fourth-of-July, Christmas-and-New-Year's best clothes, and looked as fine as fiddles. Poor Miss Morris came, with her handkerchief up to her eyes, and stayed so all the time, crying as if her heart would break, I presume. She was so dismal, in her old green barège, that Minnie kindly dressed her in Mrs. Montague's purple silk, which fitted her quite well; so she didn't look so very bad, after all. Aren't you glad? I am.

Pretty soon in came the minister, who was no other than Angelina! as her black nun's robe was the most like a gown that could be found; and when she was set up with her back against the centre table, the parlor door opened, and in marched the bride and bridegroom. Minnie and Maggie held them in their proper places, and the minister married them in rhyme; which, it strikes me, was a new style. This was what he said:

"Now you're married, you must obey;
You must be true to all you say,
And live together all your life;
And I pronounce you man and wife!"

When the marriage ceremony was over, the children set Mr. and Mrs. Morris down side by side on the sofa, and leaving them to entertain the company, and talk for themselves if they could, got the supper ready. It was such a grand supper that they were obliged to have a table from up stairs besides the dining table. Everything in the box of eatables was brought out, even the roast beef and buttered toast, two dishes not ordinarily seen at suppers. The sugar-plums were disposed around wherever room could be found, and when everything was ready, Minnie took Toby to the parlor door and made him say:

TOBY.

Ladies and gentlemens, please to come to supper,

Plum cake, and cream cake, and white bread and butter.

Up jumped Mr. Morris in such a violent hurry that he nearly tumbled over, and offered his arm to his bride; which Minnie made him do by bending it round, and pinning his kid hand fast to his waistcoat. Maggie and Lina made the rest of the company walk after them in procession, as fast as they could lift them up; and they all pranced and paraded round by the back of the house into the dining room. Only poor Miss Morris was left out, and she had tumbled off her chair, and was lying behind the piano, on the top of her head, with one leg sticking straight up in the air like an awning post, and the other foot apparently boxing her ears, as it was turned back in a most extraordinary manner, till it touched her head.

Meanwhile, there were fine times going on in the dining room. Mr. Montague took the foot of the table, and the bride and groom the head. As soon as they were all seated, Mr. Montague said:

MR. MONTAGUE. Ladies and gentlemen, don't you think we'd better drink the bride's health? Here, Toby, give the company some wine glasses.

MRS. M. Dear me, ladies, what a pity! there's only six goblets; so the rest will have to drink out of teacups!

ALL THE DOLLS (or all the three little girls, whichever you please). Oh, never mind; that doesn't make any difference.

MR. MONT. The bride, ladies and gentlemen!

ALL THE DOLLS. Mrs. Morris! hurray! hurree! hurror!

MRS. M. Now, Isabella, it's time for you to change your dress, my dear. You are going travelling, you know.

ISABELLA. Oh, what a pity! I don't want to take it off a bit!

But, of course, she had to. It wouldn't have done to go travelling in a white silk dress, would it, you dear little poppet?

So Maggie took Miss Isabella (for they called her either that or Mrs. Morris by turns, indifferently), away from table, and dressed her in her gray travelling dress, which was trimmed with black velvet and small steel buttons. Then she put on her second best bonnet, with a blue veil, and her India-rubbers, in case it should be damp, and locked up the wedding dress in her trunk, which was about as large as a candle box, had a real little lock and key, and her initials painted on the side. When she was all ready, down she came again, to take leave of her relations and friends, who had eaten up all the wooden refreshments by this time (though, strange to say, the dishes seemed as full as ever), while Minnie, Maggie, and Lina eat up the sugar plums; and poor Miss Morris sucked her thumbs, I suppose, for not a speck of anything else did she get.

There was a great time bidding good-by, and so many hard noses were bumped against the bride's cheek this time, that they made a dent, which looked quite like a dimple, and improved her appearance very much indeed. As to Mr. Morris, nobody took the slightest notice of him, as is usually the case with the bridegroom, but he didn't seem to mind it in the least; for he went on smirking at the company as blandly as ever. Perhaps he didn't want people's noses making holes in his face; you wouldn't want them made in yours, would you? you dear little Pinkey Winkey! Bless your heart! there's dimples enough in that cunning face already.

But now the carriage was brought round to the door, for Mr. and Mrs. Morris to go on their travels. It was made of—ahem!—tin, and was drawn by two dashing tin horses, with tails like comets, and manes like waterfalls, and such a great number of bright red spots painted all over them, that they looked as if they had broken out with a kind of scarlet measles.

The bride and bridegroom were put in their places, the big trunk was hoisted up in front, and away they went! and travelled all the way down the entry to the head of the stairs, and through sister Alice's room to the fireplace! My! what a long journey! 'most a hundred miles, I should think! that is, it would seem so to dolls.

Thus ended the grand play of Miss Isabella Belmont Montague's wedding, which had taken two whole afternoons to finish, and which the children thought the most interestingest play that ever was. If you want to know what became of her after that, I advise you to go right to Lina's house and ask how Mr. and Mrs. Morris come on with their housekeeping! That's all there is of this story — BOO!!

THE FAIRY WISH.

ONCE upon a time there lived a little old man, with his little old wife, in a little old house that ran on wheels. Did you ever? Well, I never did.

The reason why the little old house ran on wheels was, that the little old man used to keep a monkey show in it, and drove it about for a caravan; with an old white horse, that had a blind eye, to draw it; but now the monkeys were all dead and buried, and the little old man and woman lived all alone-ty-donty. It had bright green blinds, bright red sides, a bright blue door, and bright yellow steps. On the bright blue door there was a bright brass knocker, which was polished up at such a rate that you could see your face in it, looking as l-o-n-g as anything; and underneath that was a bright brass door plate, with the old showman's name, "Timmy Timmens," on it, which was also polished up until you could see your face in it, looking as b-r-o-a-d as anything. Did you ever? Well, I never did!

Inside there was a rag carpet of all the colors of the rainbow; a little old four-post bedstead, with a patchwork counterpane; two high-backed rocking chairs, with patchwork covers over the backs; a table with an oil cloth cover, that had a little old tea tray on it, set up against the wall; two bright brass candlesticks, and a china tea set; and in one corner was a glass cupboard, which contained the other plates and dishes. Hung against the wall over the mantlepiece was a sampler worked by Mrs. Timmy Timmens when she was a girl, which represented Noah's ark, with all the animals, of exactly the same size, done in cross stitch, in such bright grass-green worsted that it quite set your teeth on edge to look at it. Besides these, there was a little round stove, with a long stove pipe, that came out on top of the caravan, and ended with a flourishing weathercock, representing a fat old woman in a high gale, with her umbrella turned inside out; which moved when the smoke came puffing up harder than usual, and had no connection whatever with any wind that blew.

Now, Mr. Timmy Timmens and his wife, being mighty simple old people, were fond of reading fairy stories, and believed entirely in every word of them. They hadn't the smallest doubt that sprites and fairies were as common as peas this very minute, and would have thought it quite a matter of course if a wonderful gift had suddenly tumbled down the very stove pipe, or a beautiful lady come bursting through the wall, and offered to carry them off to fairy land in a mother-of-pearl chariot, drawn by milk-white doves. If a cat looked hard at her and mewed piteously, the little old woman would sigh, "Well, this is fairy work, I'll bet a crooked sixpence! She looks like an enchanted princess, poor thing! don't she, Timmy, dear?" If a donkey brayed louder than usual, and seemed more obstinate than ever before, the little old man would exclaim, "There, I told you so! an unfortunate young man, of surpassing beauty, enchanted in this dreadful shape by a wicked fairy! That's plain to be seen! No wonder he utters such cries of distress!" and then they both groaned together, and waggled their heads, and blew their noses so exactly in time with two yellow silk pocket handkerchiefs, that people thought two fishmen must be blowing their horns at once. Did you ever? Well, I never did!

One fine morning the little old man and woman went out to take a walk on the common; for the house stood right beside the road, in an empty field of scrubby grass, with no fence round it. Just behind the house, to be sure, was a paling, which enclosed a garden about as big as a good-sized dining table, where the little old man and woman grew one or two cabbages, two or three tomatuses, three or four potatuses, and four or five radishes, for their own eating; but all the rest was just open common. The old woman had a large basket in her hand, all ready to pop down over any fairies she might see lying asleep in a bluebell, and the old man was leaning heavily on his stick, as he was rather feeble, and, besides, had the rheumatism in his big toe.

"Dear me, Timmy," said the old woman, "what a good thing it would be, now, if we could only find a kind fairy who would move our house for us somewhere nearer the village. Now that poor old Dobbin is dead—killed, I've no doubt, by a wicked enchanter—we can no longer get around from place to place without stirring a step from the house; and we are so far away, that we can't walk over to take tea with any of our neighbors. Do let us keep a sharp lookout as we walk along, and see if we can't find a fairy ring or a fairy flower."

"With all my heart!" said Tim; and so they tottered along, peering very hard into all the bushes, and hurrying to examine every little patch of grass that looked greener and brighter than the rest, in the hope that it was a fairy ring. All at once, the little old man stopped short, and pointed with his stick at a beautiful spray of foxglove.

"There!" cried Mr. Timmens.

"Where?" cried Mrs. Timmens.

"Right before your eyes!" said the little old man. "Don't you see it? A fairy foxglove, as my name is Timmy Timmens!"

"My goodness gracious, stars, and what's-his-names!" cried the little old woman; "so there is! as sure as my name is Polly Timmens!"

So the little old man and woman hurried up to the flower, and after trying a great many times to stoop down, making their old joints crack like so many torpedoes, Mrs. Polly succeeded in plucking it, and off they went, pell-mell, hurry-scurry, to the little old house that ran on wheels, to consult their fairy story books, and see what was the right thing to be done in such a case! Did you ever? Well, I never did.

Down sat the little old man in his rocking chair with the patchwork cover, and down sat the little old woman in her rocking chair with thepatchwork cover; and after a long consultation of the "Sorrows of Prince Popinjay," and the "Wonderful History of the Princess Lillie Bulero and the Fairy Allinmieyeo," they discovered that the proper way to do was to hold the fairy foxglove in your hand exactly as the clock struck twelve, at noon, and say

"Rorum corum torum snoram,

Highcum tickleme cockolorum!"

seven times; then shut your eyes tight and wish, stand on one leg and turn round three times, and, presto! you would find, when you opened your eyes, that your wish was accomplished!

"Dear me!" cried Mrs. Polly Timmens when her husband had finished reading this wonderful charm; "how lucky it is that we should be the ones to find the fairy foxglove! just as we were wishing, too, for something of the sort. Let me see, it is half past eleven now, I declare! Timmy, my dear, I'll go into the garden and gather two or three tomatuses and three or four potatuses for dinner, for it would be a shame to leave our fine vegetables behind; and then, as the clock strikes twelve, we'll try the fairy spell, wish that our house was in the village, and see what comes of it."

So the little old woman, taking a small basket off a nail, and a sharp knife in her hand, went into the garden to gather the vegetables. Down she plumped beside the bed, and began to dig and cut at the potatuses to get them up. Her back was turned to the house, and the tall stalks and thick leaves of the tomato bushes quite hid it from her view when she sat on the ground, for she was a teeny-tawny little old woman. While she was thus engaged, the little old man was sitting inside with the book open in one hand, for fear he should forget the charm, and the fairy foxglove tight in the other, waiting impatiently for her return. The hands of the clock kept getting nearer and nearer to twelve, and at last there was only one moment wanting to the time.

"Why, goodness gracious me!" cried Mr. Timmy Timmens; "has Polly forgot all about the fairy wish? I declare, I have a great mind to begin alone." Just as he said these words, the clock began to strike! and at the same moment a tremendous hullabaloo arose on the road. "There come the fairies!" squeaked the little old man; and without waiting another second, he stood straight up in the middle of the floor, and said, in a trembling voice:

"Rorum corum torum snorum,

Highcum tickleme cockolorum!"

seven times over; then, shutting up his eyes as tight as possible, stood on one leg, and cried, "Please, good fairy, Polly and I wish our house was in the middle of the village!"

Hardly had he said these words, than a long red object, that looked wonderfully like a cow's tail, suddenly whisked in at the half open door; the wind caught the door, and shut it to, slam! bang! and with a jerk that made the bright brass knocker give a tremendous double knock on the bright blue door, and sent the bright tin saucepans scattering in every direction, the house started suddenly down on the road on a double-quick trot! Did you EVER?! Well, I NEVER did!!

It happened that a large drove of cows and oxen were going down to market that day, and being very hot, and tired, and thirsty, they naturally objected to being driven in that way any longer, and commenced cutting a variety of capers that were enough to frighten you out of your wits. At last one irascible little bull, who had been riding on the other ones' backs, charging at all the innocent ducks, geese, and pigs he could find on the road, and finally had tossed one of the men who were driving him right up in the air, dashed on ahead, and, seeing the little house with the bright red sides, took the color as a personal insult to himself. Down went his head and up went his heels, and in another minute he would have bounced right into poor Mr. Timmy Timmens' dwelling, when one of the drivers saw him, and rushing up, gave him a good whack with his whip. Master Bull turned round to see what was to pay; in an instant his tail was caught in the door as I told you, and, frightened half out of his wits, he galloped off, dragging the little house on wheels after him, and roaring with pain, while the drivers looked on, roaring with laughter.

Meanwhile, the little old man remained standing on one leg, not daring to open his eyes, for fear the charm would be broken, and only wishing that the little old woman were with him. At last the house stopped, moving with another jerk, that sent the little old man toppling back in his rocking chair, and a moment afterward the door was opened a little bit, and a strange voice said, "Well, here we are at the village, old gentleman, begging your pardon," and then all was silent.

Up jumped the little old man, opening his eyes very wide this time, hobbled to the door, and looked out. There, sure enough, he was, in the pleasant, shady village street, with the church directly opposite, so nice for Sundays, and nothing to be seen but a drove of cows and oxen going down the road at some distance!

"Well, was there ever anything known like this?" cried Mr. Timmy Timmens. "If this isn't the most wonderful fairy doings I ever heard of! I must go right off to find Polly, and tell her the happy news."

So saying, he went down the bright yellow steps, carefully shut the bright blue door behind him, and toddled off as fast as he could to the common.

Now the little old woman, before she had finished digging up the potatuses, found the sun very warm and herself very sleepy, and thinking her husband would be sure to call her when twelve o'clock came, she just got under the shade of the tomatuses, and went off in a nice nap. When she woke, she jumped up in a hurry, exclaiming, "Why, bless me—how could I have forgotten about twelve o'clock? I must make haste into the house this minute." But where was the house? The little old woman stared all around until she nearly stared her eyes out, but it was nowhere to be seen.

"Why, my goodness gracious, stars, and what's-his-names!" squealed the little old woman, letting fall her knife and basket; "where has the house runned to? Timmy must have tried the fairy charm without ever telling me! I mean to go right to the village and see if it is there."

So she gathered up her basket and knife, stuffed the basket, and her apron, and her pockets with all the vegetables she could carry, and started off for the village. Before she was half way there, however, she met her husband. "Where is it?" "There it is!" they called at the same moment, and falling into each other's arms and a mud puddle, they stood for a long time, saying by turns: "Did you ever?" "No, I never!" "Would you believe it?" "Not 'less I see'd it!" and then they took hold of hands and trotted off to the little house that ran on wheels.

There they found it, all high and dry, under a big apple tree, looking as nice as ninepence. With joyful hearts they hurried inside, picked up the saucepans, and cooked all the tomatuses and potatuses for dinner, with an apple dumpling for dessert, made of some of the apples that had fallen off the tree; and after that, the little old man and the little old woman, and the bright green blinds, and the bright red walls, and the bright blue door with the bright brass knocker, and the bright yellow steps, all lived in peace and the middle of the village, believing more firmly than ever in the existence of fairies, and never doubting that their house had been moved solely by the miraculous power of the fairy spell,

"Rorum corum torum snorum,

Highcum tickleme cockolorum!"

And if they're not dead they live there still! Don't you believe it? Well I NEVER did!